Phoebe's Revolt

Natalie Babbitt

Phoebe's Revolt

Farrar, Straus and Giroux

New York

For M.F.B.
with all my heart

Phoebe Euphemia Brandon Brown
    Lived in a fancy house in town.
She lived there quite alone unless
    You count Miss Trout, her governess,
The butler, cook, and maids in force,
    And Mr. and Mrs. Brown, of course,
And Phoebe's kitten Elihu
    And her Aunt Celeste, who lived there too.
Good fortune smiled on Phoebe Brown,
    But revolution brought her down.

The times (the year was nineteen-four),
   The clothes that everybody wore,
The way that people like the Browns
   Were living, in our larger towns,
And Phoebe's way of being prone
   To having notions of her own—
All these were more or less to blame
   For Phoebe's crime and Phoebe's shame.

In nineteen-four, at any rate,
    Phoebe Euphemia Brown was eight.
The trouble all began in June
    While getting dressed one afternoon.
For Phoebe, who was mostly good
    And often did the things she should,
Stepped forward in her underwear
    With mingled passion and despair
And loudly said she hated bows
    And roses on her slipper toes
And dresses made of fluff and lace
    With frills and ruffles every place
And ribbons, stockings, sashes, curls
    And *everything* to do with girls.

She said she had just one request:
    To dress the way her father dressed,
In simple white and sober black
    Unornamented front and back.

And yet the clothes that Phoebe wore
　　Were normal back in nineteen-four
And other little girls in fluff
　　All seemed to be content enough.
Unhampered by the current styles,
　　They went about with happy smiles
To picnics, teas, parades and such
　　And did not seem to mind it much.

Now Phoebe's mother tried her best
    And so did Phoebe's Aunt Celeste.
They both maintained that little girls
    Looked sweet with ribbons in their curls.
They often spoke of one such child
    Who dressed correctly, yet who smiled.
They spoke, while Phoebe made a face,
    Of Phoebe's little cousin Grace—
How mild she was, and how polite,
    How charming in her pink and white.
But "Prissy Prig" was Phoebe's name
    For little Grace, and when she came
To visit as she often did,
    Then Phoebe often ran and hid.

Well, Phoebe's mother was distressed
    And so was Phoebe's Aunt Celeste.
And poor Miss Trout, who had to stay
    With Phoebe every single day
And get her dressed and fix her hair,
    Was nearly driven to despair.
But Phoebe's father only smiled
    And said she was a novel child.

One morning at their breakfast tea
   They all were trying manfully
To disregard the wails of gloom
   That filtered down from Phoebe's room.
(Like "Do I have to put on *that?*"
   And "I don't *want* to wear a hat!"
With Miss Trout's voice, a little shrill:
   "Now, Phoebe, *please!* You *must* hold still!")
That morning, though her nerves were taut,
   Poor Phoebe's mother had a thought.

"We'll give a party! Every chum
   of Phoebe's will be sure to come
In pretty clothes. Why, then she'll see
   She's acting very foolishly.
She'll change her mind, I'm sure, Celeste,
   And want to be like all the rest."

But Phoebe's father shook his head.
   "I'm not so sure . . ." was all he said.

They planned the party anyway
    And sent out notes that very day.
The maids put flowers everywhere
    And Phoebe's mother hired a bear
That danced when certain tunes were played,
    And Cook made cakes and lemonade.

The time came round. Eight little girls
    Arrived, all ribbons, lace and curls.
And Mrs. Brown and Aunt Celeste
    Stood greeting every little guest.

But where was Phoebe? Minutes passed.
    They knew the awful truth at last
When came the voice of poor Miss Trout:
    "She's in the tub and won't get out!"

"She's in the tub and won't get out!"
    The news was whispered all about.
Phoebe's mother clutched her hair,
    Turned pale, and hurried up the stair,
And Aunt Celeste went running too,
    In hopes it wasn't really true.

But in the bathtub Phoebe sat.
    She would not move, and that was that.

There hung her dress, all pink chiffon.
　　She said she would not put it on.
They told her how her friends were dressed,
　　But Phoebe Brown was not impressed.
They told about the dancing bear.
　　She answered that she didn't care.
They mentioned shame and protocol
　　But Phoebe Brown was deaf to all.
She said, "I will not wear that dress.
　　I won't come down at all unless . . ."
She stirred the water with her toes—
　　"Unless I wear my father's clothes."

At this her mother's patience died.
    "I do not trust myself!" she cried.
She turned away and went to bed
    And wrapped cold cloths around her head,
While Auntie, with an angry cough,
    Went down and called the party off.
The guests went home without their play.
    The dancing bear was sent away.

And in the bathtub, unconsoled,
    The water slowly turning cold,
With wrinkling toes and fingertips,
    Miss Phoebe sat and chewed her lips.

The afternoon had come and gone,
    The lamps were lit, the curtains drawn,
When Phoebe's father, walking in,
    Was told about his daughter's sin.
He was a most resourceful man
    And right away he had a plan.
He fetched an armload from his room
    And went to work his daughter's doom
Where in the bathtub, cold and wet,
    That stubborn child was sitting yet.
"Hop out," he said. "The storm has passed.
    I've come to save the day at last.
You say you want to wear my clothes?
    It *is* surprising, I suppose,
But still, I've got some things to spare
    That I'd be more than glad to share."
And there they were, her just deserts:
    One of his own fine evening shirts,
A starchy collar, white cravat,
    And last of all, a tall silk hat.

Her father's clothes! And yet—somehow—
    They didn't seem so lovely now.
The charm had paled. The lure was gone.
    But Phoebe had to put them on.

Yes, Phoebe had to put them on.
    Too late for lace and pink chiffon.
She had her father's clothes instead—
    For *seven days*, her father said.
He had so nicely said she could,
    She knew she must, she felt she should.
She couldn't spurn that hat and shirt
    And have him get his feelings hurt.

So Phoebe wore her father's clothes.
    They looked peculiar, heaven knows,
But those amused by this array
    Would kindly look the other way
Or step behind a potted fern
    Till feeling more controlled and stern.

And when the seven days had passed
    And she could take them off at last,
Miss Phoebe left her father's clothes
    And reassumed her lace and bows
And never said a single word
    (At least, that anybody *heard*).

But Phoebe's father poked around
    In trunks and boxes till he found
A faded picture framed in pearl,
    The picture of a little girl;
A little girl dressed head to toe
    In funny clothes from long ago
And on her face an awful frown.
    That little girl was Mrs. Brown
And eighteen-eighty was the date,
    The year that Mrs. Brown was eight.
He brought it down and let it stand
    Demurely on the parlor grand.

And what did Mrs. Brown do then?
    She turned away and took her pen
And wrote her seamstress on the spot:
    "Please come at once—I quite forgot—
My daughter Phoebe needs a dress,
    In broadcloth or in serge, I guess—
A simple sailor dress or two
    In sober, modest navy blue.
And when you're done, and if you're free,
    You might make one or two for me."

Phoebe Euphemia Brandon Brown
    Lived in a fancy house in town.
She dressed in ruffles, chin to hem,
    When circumstance demanded them,
But otherwise and normally
    She dressed much more informally.